Wizards
OF WAVERLY PLACE

All Mixed Up

Adapted by Heather Alexander

Based on the series created by Todd J. Greenwald

Part One is based on the episode "The Supernatural," Written by Matt Goldman

Part Two is based on the episode "Alex's Spring Fling," Written by Matt Goldman

𝒟𝒾𝓈𝓃𝑒𝓎 PRESS

New York

PART
ONE

Chapter One

Justin Russo couldn't stop staring at her.

Her long, silky blond hair shimmered in the afternoon sun. Her aquamarine eyes were the color of the Caribbean Sea, and when she smiled, her face lit up brightly. She was *beyond* gorgeous.

What he wouldn't do to have her notice him just once!

I'd give up my mint-condition collector

G.I. Joe doll, Justin thought. In fact, he'd give away his entire collection of prized superhero figures to go out with her. But he knew that wasn't going to happen. *Ever.*

"Dude, close your mouth. Your tongue is going to dry out," his friend Henry joked.

Justin suddenly realized his mouth had dropped wide open! He took a swig of water from his water bottle and opened his textbook, trying to look as if he were doing something. Something other than staring at her.

"Listen, man." Henry nudged him. "Why don't you just ask her out?"

"Kari *Langsdorf*?" Justin gaped at his friend in disbelief. "I can't ask out Kari Langsdorf! She has no idea who I am. She's never even talked to me. I'm totally invisible to her."

Justin turned his gaze again to Kari. She stood by the front door of Tribeca Prep. A bunch of guys swarmed around her. He could hear her giggle. He leaned in closer, hoping to overhear what made her laugh. Suddenly, his shoulder was shoved by a guy walking past.

"Sorry, man." The guy grinned. "I didn't see you there."

"Why would you?" he muttered. It was the story of his life—*especially* his life in high school. "Totally invisible to everyone," Justin told Henry.

Justin watched the guy walk right up to Kari. No hesitation at all. Why would he hesitate? Justin reminded himself. The guy was a high school senior and looked like he belonged in the starring role in a teen movie on TV. He was the kind of guy girls like Kari noticed.

"Hey, Kari." The guy smiled, revealing perfect white teeth. "You want to check out a movie this weekend?"

"Do you play baseball?" she asked.

The cute guy raised his eyebrows. "No. But I'm quarterback of the football team, president of the student council, *and* I'm a swimsuit model."

"Oh." Kari seemed unimpressed. "I only date baseball players." She shrugged her shoulders and walked away from him.

Justin stared in surprise. If Kari wouldn't pay attention to that guy, he knew he should never think about even approaching her. Then he noticed that she was heading in his direction. She was coming his way! *Closer* . . . he had trouble breathing . . . *closer* . . . and then she bumped into him!

"Oh! Sorry." She blinked rapidly, as if confused. "Didn't see you there."

Justin choked out a chuckle as she walked right past him.

Henry gave him a friendly shove. "So, Justin." He wiggled his eyebrows suggestively. "Do you play baseball?"

Justin watched Kari walk toward the parking lot. "Yes," he said with a sigh.

For Kari, he'd play baseball. For Kari, he'd play *anything*. He would be a baseball superstar!

"Are you going to try out for the team this year?" Henry asked.

"I might." Justin sniffed at the faint scent of her perfume still floating in the air.

Henry gave Justin a serious look. "Think you got a shot at making it?"

Justin sighed again, reality crashing down around him. He stunk at playing baseball. "Absolutely not."

Chapter Two

Alex Russo stood behind the counter of the Waverly Sub Station, the restaurant that her parents owned and ran. She was thinking about the essay she had to write for English class. Then she thought about next Tuesday's math test. She knew she should probably go upstairs to her family's apartment and hit the books, but that sounded so . . . boring. She thought about the cute boys who sometimes hung out at the restaurant after school. Homework could definitely wait.

"Hey, Alex," her best friend, Harper Evans, called out. She hurried over to the counter. "Can I get a turkey sandwich?"

Alex shook her head. "I'm off the clock." She gestured to the kitchen behind her. "You know where everything is," she told her.

"Well, if you're off the clock, then what are we doing here?" Harper demanded. "I've got a jean jacket at home that's not going to sequin itself."

Alex smiled. Her friend loved do-it-yourself fashion. "Relax, Harper. We're just waiting for my dad to come back with the team he's coaching, so we can see the cute guys."

The girls turned as the door to the restaurant suddenly swung open. A group of boys in red-and-black baseball shirts that had AZTECS printed on the front headed into the sandwich shop.

"All right, guys," called Mr. Russo. "Root beer floats are on the house." He grinned. He loved sports, especially baseball, and he really loved coaching.

The team cheered and grabbed chairs at the few empty tables.

Mr. Russo noticed his younger son, Max, playing video games in the corner, and he waved him over. "Hey, Justin tried out for the first time and made the team." He proudly pointed to Justin in his brand-new uniform. "Who knew?" Mr. Russo was totally surprised that Justin was into baseball. He'd always thought Justin was more interested in hitting the books than in playing sports.

Justin blushed as his dad beamed at him. "Well, I know how much you love baseball, so I figured I'd, um, give it a shot."

Max's eyes lit up. "Awesome! Then it's settled. I'm the Aztecs' number one fan. Let the trash talking begin." He chuckled, already planning ways to tease his older brother.

Justin rolled his eyes. "Dad, he's doing it again."

Mr. Russo placed his arm around his younger son's shoulder. "Uh, Maxy, we really appreciate the enthusiasm, but let's not revisit what happened on the soccer field."

Max tried playing innocent. "What soccer field?"

"The one the park police said you can't go to anymore," his dad said.

"Excuse me for cheering for my brother. Is that a crime?" Max asked.

"According to the park police, yes." His dad was no longer smiling.

Max shook his head. Why did no one understand the art of being a committed fan? You couldn't hold back. You needed energy, heart, and a lot of devious creativity—his specialty. "The kid in the diaper started it," Max reminded his dad.

Alex ignored her father's conversation with Max. She was fixated on the cute guy with the curly brown hair also wearing the Aztecs uniform. His name was Riley, and Alex had had a crush on him for a long time. They had gone out on a date once, but that had turned into a total disaster. But Alex was determined to go out with him again. She tried to act cool as he approached the counter.

"Hey, Alex, do you have an extra-long spoon?" Riley asked.

Alex took a deep breath. "Sure," she said casually. She smiled and walked calmly into the kitchen.

Spoon, spoon, long-handled spoon . . . Alex pulled open drawer after drawer. No spoon here. Nothing in there. She tossed a pile of spoons out of another drawer, and they clattered to the floor. She slammed the drawer shut. She had to find the spoon—fast. She discovered a basket of silverware in a cabinet and dumped it onto the counter with a crash. A long-handled spoon. Perfect!

Alex grabbed it, smoothed her dark hair, and calmly walked back to the counter. "Here you go, Riley." She handed him the spoon, giving him a wide smile.

Riley looked at her oddly, having heard all the clattering and crashing. "Uh, thanks."

"What was that?" Harper asked, after Riley returned to his table. "I thought you were off the clock."

"I'm always on the clock for Riley," Alex said dreamily. "Isn't he *so* cute?"

"You mean Justin," Harper corrected her. Harper had had a crush on Alex's older brother since they were in elementary school.

"No, Riley." Sometimes Alex wondered if Harper needed her eyes checked. Riley was cute. Her brother was *so* not.

"Justin's cute," Harper insisted.

Alex chose to ignore her. Harper's crush on

Justin made her question just how silly her friend really could be. She looked over at Riley's table. "I can't believe Justin's on Riley's team. Finally, after years of Justin being a bore, I can use him for my own personal gain."

Harper leaned closer. "How are you going to do that?"

"I have no idea," Alex admitted. "But it's a nice feeling, the kind that makes you stop and give thanks you have a brother." Alex would have thought that having a brother two years older than her would have worked to her advantage long before now. But Justin wasn't that kind of brother. Usually, he was the annoying kind. Oh, well, better late than never, Alex thought.

"Here he comes!" Harper squealed, spotting Justin heading toward them. "How do I look?"

Alex checked out Harper's red-and-white dress, red-and-white headband, and red-and-white dangling earrings. Harper definitely had a thing about matching. "Fine," Alex replied.

Harper's eyes widened in horror. "Just *fine*? Fine isn't good enough!" She glanced at Justin. "Oh, shoot! Shoot! Shoot!" She bolted toward the door.

Alex sighed. Harper could be such a drama queen!

"Hey," Justin said to Alex.

"Hey, Justin. Congrats on making the team Riley's on. Baseball, right?" Alex asked.

Justin frowned. "Yep. I made the team all right."

"Well, you don't sound 'all right,'" Alex commented. "What's the matter?"

Justin glanced behind him. Then he grabbed his sister's arm and dragged her back into the kitchen. "I've done a bad, bad thing, Alex," he admitted.

"What?" Alex asked.

Justin took a deep breath. He knew Alex would be the only one to understand. "I charmed the baseball so Dad would think I'm a good pitcher."

"I didn't know you were into baseball," Alex said. Her brother usually spent more time in the library than on the baseball field.

"I'm not. I'm into Kari Langsdorf," he confided.

"Okay. So what's the bad, bad thing you did?" Alex asked.

"I cheated. I used magic to make the baseball team. If Dad knew, he would flip out." Justin was a wizard. He could do magic. Alex and Max were wizards, too. They came from a family of wizards, but no one—not even their best friends—knew. It was a big secret. If people found out about their powers, they'd probably be locked up in a lab somewhere with weird scientists poking at them. They had promised their dad they would never use magic, except when he taught them magic classes in their basement. But Justin had broken his promise.

"Hmmm." Alex never thought twice about using magic out in the real world. Doing spells was fun, so why not enjoy it? Of course, the problems came when her magic backfired— which was just about always. Spells were a lot harder than just waving a wand and making things magically appear. "Yeah, but the important thing is now you're on the baseball team with Riley," she reminded Justin. She liked to look on the bright side of things. This could definitely work out to her advantage!

"What?" Justin asked, following her.

"Well, Riley's the catcher, so he can teach you some stuff," Alex explained. "But until then, you should probably use magic to stay on the team."

"Alex, I'm not like you. I don't break the rules. I'm ridden with guilt. It's eating up my insides." He clutched his stomach. "Pretty soon I'll be just a shell."

"Ugh. You'll get over it." Alex rolled her

eyes. She needed Justin to stay on the team, so she'd have a reason to hang out at practices and games, and cozy up to Riley. Justin was her *in*. "And, Justin"—she decided to try logic—"magic is your talent. Why should a wizard not use magic?" Alex asked.

Justin thought about it. Maybe she *did* have a point. But he hated lying to his dad. . . .

"Hey, congratulations on making the team," a voice behind him suddenly said.

Justin looked up and nearly stopped breathing. It was her!

"I'm Kari," she said, smiling at him.

"Hi, Kari." He was totally stunned! "I'm Just-Just— I'm Just—"

"Just so happy to meet you," Alex said, coming to her brother's rescue. "Yes, he is. And his name is Justin."

Justin chuckled and nodded vigorously.

"Well, it's nice to meet you, Justin. I love going to baseball games, so I'm sure we'll be seeing a lot of each other." She smiled again. "I *love* baseball."

"Uh-huh." Justin tried to speak, but he was so nervous! He laughed awkwardly again as Kari waved and headed back across the sandwich shop.

"She can see me," he said to Alex, totally amazed that his baseball jersey had so much power. He didn't even have to use magic! "She can totally see me. I'm not invisible anymore."

Alex gasped. "No way! You know the invisibility spell? I'll trade you for the popularity spell."

Justin's little sister didn't get it. But he did. Suddenly his choice was crystal clear. "You know what? I am *totally* going to use magic. Thanks, Alex. You always know the right *wrong* thing to do."

Alex smiled. Excellent! She gave Justin a nudge toward the table of baseball players. "Now go sit by Riley and tell him how cool I am," she told him.

Chapter Three

Justin glanced up at the scoreboard at Lynch Memorial Field. The game was so close. He watched the player on the pitcher's mound and was happy that it wasn't him standing there. He liked sitting on the bench. He got to wear the uniform, Kari liked him because he was on the team, and he didn't have to go near a baseball. Perfect.

"Here we go! Come on now!" his dad called from the dugout.

The pitcher threw the ball high into the air.

"Ball four!" yelled the umpire. "Take your base!"

Justin cringed as the batter jogged to first base.

"Time, Ump!" Mr. Russo called.

"Time!" The umpire agreed to the time-out.

His dad signaled to Justin. It was his turn now. He would have to pitch the rest of the game. Justin jogged over to the mound.

"Nice job today. Nice job." Mr. Russo patted the other pitcher on the back as the player left the mound. He turned to his son. "All right, Justin. Let's see if you can finish this thing."

"Yay, Justin!" Harper screamed. She nudged the man sitting in the stands next to her and pointed to the pitcher. "He and I are going to be going out soon," she confided to the stranger.

Then she stood up and walked over to Alex

by the fence behind home plate. "Justin looks great in his uniform," Harper told her.

Alex wrinkled her nose. "He slept in it last night."

Harper sighed. "I find that totally attractive." She thought about Justin snuggled up in his uniform. How adorable!

It's all up to me, Justin thought. He closed his eyes as a line of sweat trickled down his forehead. He was nervous. Really nervous.

Justin opened his eyes and tried to focus on Riley's open catcher's mitt. He wound up and pitched. The ball zigzagged wildly, bouncing off the fence and landing in the dirt behind the catcher. Riley shook his head in amazement. He pulled off his mask and went to scoop it up.

Harper nudged her friend. "Alex, here comes Riley! Do you want to talk to him alone?"

"That'd be nice." Alex fluffed her long, wavy hair.

"Got it. If you need me, I'll be over here." She pointed to the stands. She turned and saw Justin looking their way. "Hi, Justin!" she cried, waving. She smiled broadly. Maybe Justin will come over to talk to me, too, she thought.

Alex glanced up as Riley walked behind home plate. She pretended to be surprised to see him, which she thought was kind of lame, since he was the catcher and the catcher always stood near home plate. Oh, well. "Hey, Riley. Cute uniform."

Riley beamed. "Thanks. It was my idea to go with the sleeveless jerseys." He showed off the red jersey layered over his black long-sleeved shirt.

Alex smiled mysteriously. "I'm going to be your good-luck charm."

"What?" Riley stepped closer to the fence. He gave Alex a curious look.

"Whenever I'm here, you'll win," Alex explained matter-of-factly.

Riley smirked. He pointed to the batter from the opposing team. "If this guy strikes out, I'll believe you."

"You'll see," Alex said confidently. Then she walked casually toward Harper. She could feel Riley staring at her, but she didn't turn back around. This was all part of her get-Riley-to-ask-me-out plan. She was trying to play it cool.

Meanwhile, Mr. Russo headed out to the pitcher's mound to talk to Justin. He tried to look upbeat. He didn't want to pressure his son. He reminded himself that winning wasn't everything. But it *was* nice—and he really wanted his team to win.

"Get this guy out and we win," Mr. Russo said. "If you don't, we lose."

Justin inhaled deeply. He felt like he might be sick.

"No pressure," his dad said.

Yeah, right, Justin thought. He watched his dad walk back to the sidelines. He watched the batter take a few practice swings. He stared at Riley and squatted down, his catcher's mitt wide open. Suddenly, Riley's mitt looked so far away. Justin knew he was in deep trouble.

"Come on, Justin! Good luck, Justin!" Kari jumped up and down in the stands. "Yay!"

Justin watched Kari cheer for him. His stomach was in knots.

"Come on, Justin!" Max called, sitting next to Kari. "Mow this guy down! He ain't no hitter! He couldn't hit it if you threw a basket-ball!"

The older guy sitting beside Max whirled around. "Hey, kid, do you mind? That's my son."

Max sneered. "Oh, I'm sorry . . . for *you*!" he taunted.

Back on the mound, Justin took a deep breath. Everyone was watching him. Waiting to see him strike out this guy. And that was never going to happen without using magic. I have no choice, he reasoned.

"Tomnoo Nankenesis," he chanted quietly as he pointed to the ball in his mitt. The ball glowed magically. Then Justin exhaled and let it fly.

The baseball zipped by the stunned batter. The crowd cheered.

"Strike one!" called the umpire.

"That's my brother! I'm his brother!" Max boasted. "Together we'll send you losers home!" he yelled to the opposing team.

Mr. Russo clapped his hands together. "Nice work, son! Bringing the heat!"

Justin wound up, and the ball curved across the plate. The batter swung wildly, missing completely.

"Strike two!" announced the umpire.

Mr. Russo couldn't believe his eyes. Justin was on fire! "Amazing, huh?" he said to the players on the bench. He chuckled.

Max jumped to his feet. He raised a huge megaphone to his mouth and bellowed,

"You feel that heat, losers?"

Justin winced. Max was being way too loud—and obnoxious. He fired off another pitch, faster than the other two.

"Strike three!" the umpire called. "You're out! Game over!"

The crowd whooped and stamped their feet. Mr. Russo pumped his fist in the air. Justin had pulled it off. "Nice!" he shouted.

Max was on a roll and continued to trash-talk the other team. "Way to go, loser!" he yelled to the other team. "You should change your first name to 'Lou' and your last name to 'Ser'! Get it? Loser!"

Mr. Russo rubbed his hands together and stared at the scoreboard. "Oh, boy! You ever see a kid pitch like that?" he asked himself. Then he thought about it. Justin wasn't throwing high-school pitches. Justin was throwing major-league all-star pitches. Come to think of it, I've never seen a kid pitch like that. Something's not right, he said to himself. He eyed Justin suspiciously.

After the game, Justin walked home with Kari. He couldn't believe his luck. He was sure every guy in New York City was jealous. They walked together down Waverly Place, the street where his family lived and worked.

"You were awesome out there today," Kari cooed. "Those batters had no clue what you were throwing at them. It's like they had never seen pitches before."

Justin acted as if it were no big deal. "Well, that's just what I do." He puffed out his chest. "Give them a little pop-goes-the-weasel."

"Pop-goes-the-weasel?" Kari asked curiously. "Is that like a baseball term?"

"Yeah," Justin fibbed. "In Taiwan. Where I learned the pitch."

Kari nodded, impressed. "I'm glad we finally met." She gently touched his arm. "See you around." She smiled and walked away.

Justin stared, openmouthed. He couldn't believe how this day had turned out! He smiled to himself.

"Justin, I need to talk to you." His father suddenly appeared at his side.

Justin had a bad feeling about this. "As my dad, or as my coach?" he asked.

"As your *magic* teacher." His dad looked disappointed. "You broke the rules. You never break the rules."

Justin sighed. "Alex told me to use magic."

"Here's some advice," his dad told him sternly. "Stop listening to your sister."

Justin nodded, pulled out his phone, and pretended to type. "Got it. E-mail to self. Stop listening to evil sister." He glanced at his dad. Was he in the mood for jokes? Not so much, Justin realized.

"Justin, I'm very disappointed in you. You've always been a stickler for the rules."

"All right, fine. I'll quit the team." Justin figured he'd own up to his punishment before his dad could even give it.

"No, you're not quitting the team," his dad said. "You're going to learn your lesson by pitching without magic."

"I'll get creamed!" Justin protested.

"Exactly. That's the learning-your-lesson part," Mr. Russo replied.

Justin buried his head in his hands. Parents sometimes had such cruel senses of humor. Without using magic, there was no way that he'd be able to pitch even *one* inning. I'm doomed, he thought. I'm totally doomed.

Chapter Four

Mr. Russo excitedly put on his Aztecs baseball cap and grabbed two bottles of water from the refrigerator in their apartment. The Russos were headed to another one of Justin's baseball games, and Mr. Russo was pumped.

"I'm ready for Justin's second game," Max announced from the hall next to the kitchen.

Mr. Russo turned around and laughed. Max was waving a foam finger the size of his head. It said #1 FAN.

"Uh, Max, don't you think that foam finger's a little big?" Alex asked. She sat on the orange family room sofa, flipping through a textbook.

"No." Max hurried back into his bedroom. He appeared a moment later with an even bigger foam finger. "But this one might be."

His dad smiled. He had to give his son points for team spirit. "Hey, if it rains, you can mop up the infield for us."

Max laughed. "That's a good one, Dad." He poked his dad in the stomach with his foam finger. Then he gathered both foam fingers, several pennants, a banner, and a megaphone, and followed his father out the door to head to the game. They both wanted to get there early—Mr. Russo to figure out the lineup now that the team was pitching without using magical powers, and Max to plan the best ways to psych out the other team.

Harper hurried through the front door as

they were leaving. "Hey, Alex, are you ready to go to the game?" she asked. She looked at Alex's outfit skeptically. She would have thought her friend would be more dressed up if she was planning on seeing Riley. "Come on."

Alex casually paged through her book. "Nope. I'm not going today."

"But you're Riley's good luck charm," Harper pointed out.

Alex stood up and tossed the book onto the sofa. "Well, my dad's making Justin pitch, even though he can't use a spell."

"Spell?" Harper repeated.

As soon as she said it, Alex knew she'd made a huge mistake. No one could know about their magical powers. Not even Harper.

Think fast, Alex told herself. She tossed her hair back and smiled. "Yeah, Justin had a *spelling* test and he couldn't practice pitching." She nodded. Good save! "Yeah, that works.

Nice." She turned back to Harper. "So he's going to get clobbered, and the team's going to lose."

Harper wasn't really following what Alex was saying. Since when did Alex care about the baseball team winning or losing? "But don't you want to see Riley?" she asked.

"Yes, but not if they're going to lose," Alex explained. "That's just going to show Riley that I'm not his good luck charm."

"But he might wish you were there," Harper said.

"I know. That's the good part." Alex smiled. "I won't be there, which will reinforce the idea that I *am* his good luck charm."

"*Okay*," Harper said in confusion. She still didn't get it. "But I think it would be fun to see Riley."

Alex took a deep breath and pulled Harper next to her on the sofa. "Let me explain this to you slowly. . . ."

Meanwhile, at the ballpark, Justin stood on the mound and threw horrible pitch after horrible pitch. The outfielders watched in disbelief as ball after ball meteored out of the park. The other team racked up home runs while the home crowd groaned, and soon many of the spectators left the ball field. The game was too painful to watch.

During the middle of the eighth inning, Riley called for a time-out. He jogged to the pitcher's mound to talk with Justin. He looked upset.

"Let me ask you something," Riley began.

"I know, I know. I'm getting creamed out here." Justin wasn't going to pretend it was any better than it was. But he hoped Riley had some great advice to turn the game around.

"Right, right." Riley glanced toward the few remaining fans in the stands. "Hey, does your sister ever ask about me?"

Justin groaned. Riley had no baseball advice to share. He just liked Alex. Figures!

The game seemed to drag on forever, but finally, it was over. Justin was silent as he and his dad trudged home.

When they entered the Sub Station, Mr. Russo tried to be positive. "I know it was tough going today, Justin."

"Tough going?" Justin cried. "I gave up twenty-six runs! Their guys kept running around and around and around and around—"

"Justin," Mr. Russo interrupted. "Listen." He sat his son down at a table. "Only one of my kids is going to be able to keep his powers. I don't want you relying on magic, because you might not have it one day."

Justin thought about this. In wizard families, all kids received special powers at age twelve. They spent the next six years learning how to do spells and control their magic. But the tricky part was that only one child in each family was allowed to keep his or her powers when he or she became an adult. And it was kind of a roll of the dice—there was no telling who would end up with their powers. Until now, Justin had always assumed it would be him. Alex and Max never seemed to be real competition. Was he wrong?

"All right, all right. I get it." But just because Justin understood, it still didn't make defeat any easier. "I never liked baseball anyway," he admitted.

"Then why did you try out for the team?" his dad asked.

Justin figured he might as well tell the truth. The day couldn't get any more embarrassing. "To impress Kari Langsdorf," he said.

"Oh. I get it," his dad said with a grin. "You know, when I was your age, I tried using magic to impress a girl. Turned into a *total* disaster."

"What happened?" Justin asked.

"I married her!" Mr. Russo exclaimed,

laughing at his joke. "Just kidding," he said seriously. "The point is, using magic is cheating. And cheating to impress people ultimately fails. So I suggest you practice hard, because I've decided to pitch you again next game."

"What?" Justin asked incredulously. How could his father be so cruel? he wondered. Wasn't today humiliating enough? "Dad, without magic, I'll get creamed again!" he protested.

"Not necessarily. You have some of my natural ability. We just have to find it." Mr. Russo had always been a great baseball player as a kid. There is no way Justin hasn't inherited a sliver of my talent, he thought to himself. Right?

Justin saw the gleam in his father's eyes. He knew there was no turning back. "Do I have a choice?" he asked grumpily.

"No," Mr. Russo answered. "Look, you

made a commitment, and now you have to stick to it."

"You think I can do better than today?" Justin asked hopefully.

"It'd be hard to do worse," his dad pointed out.

Even if he pitched blindfolded, Justin agreed—it couldn't be any worse than what happened at today's game. Maybe I'll go to the park and practice this week, he thought. "All right, all right, fine. I'll give it a shot."

"And no magic, right?" his dad reminded him.

"No magic," Justin replied. "Got it."

Chapter Five

"You see? They lost," Alex explained to Harper a few minutes later. She leaned on the counter at the Waverly Sub Station. "So if I had gone to the game, I couldn't possibly be Riley's good luck charm. And then he wouldn't be interested in me. Do you understand?"

Harper nodded. She took a bite of the slice of chocolate cake she was sharing with Alex. "Oh, I get it. Good plan." She glanced at the door and watched the members of the baseball team file in. Everyone looked miserable. "Now, let's talk about something that's really important. Your brother's baseball uniform." She smiled at a defeated-looking Justin. "How cute is he in that?"

Ugh! Alex thought. Harper is so gross! This crush that her best friend had on her brother was getting *really* old. Alex decided to focus her attention on Riley. And he was heading right toward her!

"Alex, where were you today?" Riley asked. "We got smeared."

Alex reached for her fork and pretended to be fascinated by the slice of cake in front of her. "Oh, I've been studying," she said casually.

Harper grinned and nudged Riley. "She wasn't there. And you lost. Sounds like she's your good-luck charm." She gave him a meaningful stare. Then Harper leaned across the counter and whispered, "You're welcome," to Alex.

Alex shot Harper a menacing look. She smiled sweetly at Riley "I'm sorry, Riley. I didn't know you wanted me to come to every game."

"Uh, yeah. You're our good-luck charm. And we need good luck at every game," he said.

"Every game?" Alex wrinkled her nose. She took a bite of cake and chewed thoughtfully. "I don't know." She could see Riley getting anxious. Her plan was working!

"I'll tell you what," Riley told her. "If you come to our next game and we win, I'll take you to the Fall Dance."

Alex felt her heart flutter, but she tried to remain calm. She knew she had to play it cool. "And what makes you think I want to go to the Fall Dance with you?"

"Every girl does, don't they?" Riley asked, brushing his brown curls off his forehead.

He had a point, Alex thought. "Yeah, you're right. Okay, you got a deal."

"Great, because I'm very superstitious.

But with you, I got a feeling we'll go all the way to the state championship."

"*And* all the way to the Fall Dance," Alex reminded him. "See ya," she called as he walked back to his table. She couldn't wait to go to the dance with Riley! I can wear that awesome shimmery copper-colored skirt I just bought, she decided. It will match his eyes *perfectly*.

Harper smiled. She was so excited for Alex. But then she frowned. "Wait. What are you going to do if Justin pitches badly at the next game, they lose, and Riley realizes you're not his good luck charm?"

"As long as I have something to do with it," Alex said confidently, "I'm pretty sure Justin's team will win the next game."

Alex used her hand to shield her eyes from the bright Saturday afternoon sun and kept her eyes focused on Justin. She was waiting for just the right moment. If she acted too early people might get suspicious. Too late and she risked running out of time before racking up the necessary runs.

Justin's pitch barely made it across the plate. Ball!

"Oh, come on, Justin!" Max yelled from the stands. "I didn't paint my face for a tied-up game!" The red paint on his face was starting to itch. He turned to the guy next to him. "This stuff is starting to burn." He tried not to panic. "Is that bad?"

The guy just shrugged.

Harper sat next to Alex in the stands. "I sure hope Justin gets out of this jam, otherwise you're not Riley's good luck charm. And I was up half the night with my mom trying to figure this out. Because when you're there, he wins, and when you're not, he doesn't."

"Don't worry," Alex assured her. "I know Justin will get out of this."

Justin pitched again. This time the ball flew

so high it grazed the batter's helmet. The guy walked, and the crowd groaned loudly. Things weren't looking good.

The other team's star hitter approached the plate. This guy had already hit three home runs against Justin.

Justin aimed the ball toward home plate. The batter connected easily and the ball rose high in the air, an obvious home run.

Now's the time, Alex decided. She pointed to the baseball soaring over the center fielder's head and quietly chanted, *"Tomnoo Nankenisis."*

There was a quick flash of light, barely noticeable to anyone on the field. Then, suddenly, the baseball reversed direction and nose-dived directly into the center fielder's mitt! He looked at the ball in amazement.

"Batter's out of there!" the umpire called. The crowd jumped up excitedly, cheering for the unbelievable catch.

Mr. Russo definitely didn't believe what

he had just seen. He stared at the batter suspiciously. But maybe, just maybe, that kid caught the ball on his own, he thought.

The Aztecs jogged into the dugout to get their turn at bat.

"Good job! Good job!" Mr. Russo cheered, patting his team on their backs.

"Thanks, Coach," Riley said.

Mr. Russo pulled Justin aside. "Uh, Justin? Is there something you want to tell me?"

"No." Justin stared meaningfully at his father. "Is there something you want to tell *me*?" Justin knew *he* hadn't used magic. Had his dad?

"No," Mr. Russo said.

"All right," Justin said.

There was an awkward silence.

"Good talk. Good talk. Let's play some ball!" Mr. Russo sent Riley up to bat.

Riley concentrated and then solidly connected his bat with the ball. The ground ball headed straight for the shortstop's open mitt.

"*Tomnoo Nankenisis,*" Alex repeated.

The ball oddly swerved around the short-stop's feet, rolling into the outfield. The player scratched his head in surprise. Riley ran to first base. The crowd cheered and Max went wild, waving his foam finger.

Something's definitely going on here, Mr. Russo realized. "Time, Ump," he called.

The umpire looked confused. A coach usually saved his time-outs for when the team was in trouble. Not when they had a man on base. "Time!" the umpire agreed.

"Justin." His dad waved him off the bench.

"You're calling a time-out to talk to a guy sitting on the bench?" the umpire asked incredulously.

"There's no rule against it!" Mr. Russo countered. Sure, it was strange, but this game had been nothing but odd so far.

The umpire frowned.

Justin stood next to his dad. "I told you, I didn't do it," he said defensively.

"I know, I know. I was watching you. There's something going on, so I want you to use your powers to counteract it and keep the game fair," he said.

"Okay," Justin replied, unsure of how he was going do this. But he knew his dad wouldn't be able to. Mr. Russo had had to give up his powers when he married his wife, a mortal. It was one of the many wizard-world rules. But his dad always said love was worth it. Justin scanned the infield. He wondered if his dad was wishing for his powers back now, though.

"Time-in," Mr. Russo told the umpire.

The umpire sighed. "Play ball!" he called.

The next batter for the Aztecs took a few practice swings, then readied himself at the plate. Alex watched the pitcher wind up and zoom a fastball. There was absolutely no way the batter would ever hit it.

Alex pointed toward the ball. *"Tomnoo Nankenisis,"* she said, slowing the ball to almost a standstill. The batter had plenty of time to connect with the ball, sending it soaring into the infield.

Justin pressed his nose against the fence separating the dugout from the field. *"Tomnoo Nankenisis,"* he chanted. The ball slowed and turned, heading for the shortstop's mitt.

Alex groaned. She was having trouble changing the direction of the ball. She had to do something else. *"Tomnoo Nankenisis,"* she repeated, speeding up the ball so quickly that it flew right through the shortstop's mitt and out the other side of the leather.

The crowd groaned. The shortstop almost fainted in surprise, staring at the searing hole in his mitt, as the ball rolled farther into the outfield. Mr. Russo gasped in horror.

Riley, meanwhile, ran around the bases. As he rounded third, the left fielder scooped up the ball. Alex bit her lip. She needed Riley to score so the team would win. *"Tomnoo Nankenisis,"* she chanted. Magically, home plate moved up the third-base line!

Justin didn't miss a beat. *"Tomnoo Nankenisis."* he said. The home plate slid back to its original spot as Riley raced toward it.

Alex gasped. What was Justin doing? The left fielder threw the ball toward the catcher. *"Tomnoo Nankenisis,"* she said again, and the base moved closer to Riley. But Riley didn't see the base shift. He darted past it and did a double take. He scooted back as the catcher caught the ball. Alex moved the base one way. Justin moved it the other. Riley danced helplessly in circles as the catcher chased him with the ball.

Finally, Riley managed to touch the base with his toe.

"Safe!" yelled the umpire.

The stands were completely silent. No one knew what to say. How could they? They weren't quite sure what they had seen. Even Max was totally speechless.

Then Kari began to laugh and cheer loudly. The crowd shook themselves out of their daze and cheered along with her.

Mr. Russo let out a deep breath. This isn't good, he thought. "Uh, time-out, Ump! Time-out!"

"Time!" the umpire agreed.

Mr. Russo headed toward the stands, pulling Justin along with him. "Alex, get over here!" he bellowed.

"You're calling a time-out to talk to a fan?" the umpire asked. Now *that's* a first, he thought.

"Show me the rule, Ump!" Mr. Russo challenged. "Show me the rule!"

The umpire grunted. He didn't know if any rule actually existed.

Alex hesitantly approached her dad. He looked really upset.

"I know what you are doing, young lady, and I want it to stop," her dad told her.

Alex sighed. "I was just trying to help."

Mr. Russo groaned. Then he pulled a notepad and pencil out of his back pocket. He scribbled a word on the paper and held it up to Justin. "Here, Justin, recite this spell."

"What is it?" Justin asked.

"It will erase everyone's memory, so they won't remember what happened in the past few minutes," his dad explained.

"Even ours?" Justin asked.

"I don't know. I don't remember. I've never used it," his dad admitted.

"All right." Justin hoped his dad knew what he was doing. "Um, *Cerebellumerasis*," he said.

Suddenly, a strange blue aura covered the stadium. Everything shimmered and glowed. Justin held his breath. Would the spell work?

Chapter Six

A few moments later, the baseball field stopped glowing.

"What just happened?" Alex asked.

Everyone in the stands looked totally confused. Then Max spotted the scoreboard. "We won! We won!" He cheered and pumped his fists in the air. "In your face, losers! Go home and cry, you little babies! I smell smoke, because you were burned!" he taunted the other teams' fans. "Whoo!"

The father of the other team's pitcher—the kid Max had been trash-talking the entire game—marched toward Max. Two security guards followed. "There he is!" the man called.

Oh, no! Max thought. He dodged around the crowd, running toward the exit.

"Get him! Get him!" the man yelled. They chased after Max. But he was long gone.

Justin felt as if he were in a fog. "Dad, I don't remember how the game ended," he said.

His dad tried to focus. He looked at the field, then the scoreboard. Nothing came to mind. "Neither do I," he admitted. "I think Alex had something to do with it." He noticed that Justin was holding something. "What's that piece of paper?" he asked, reaching over to grab it. "Hey!" A memory-erasing spell, in his handwriting. But he didn't remember writing it. Weird. He put it in his pocket. "This could come in handy someday," he told Justin.

A little while later, Alex walked home with Riley. They talked about the game until they reached Waverly Place.

"So, Alex, it looks like I've got a date for the Fall Dance," Riley said.

"Yes, you do," Alex agreed. "And Friday night, too."

Riley seemed confused. "We're going out Friday night?"

"Yeah, you asked me right after you scored the winning run," Alex fibbed. "Don't you remember?"

She could see Riley searching his brain, trying unsuccessfully to recall this piece of information. "Uh, yeah. Sure. Great." He was too embarrassed to tell her he couldn't remember. It was easier just to go with it. "Looking forward to Friday night," he said with a smile.

"Yes, you are." Alex gave him a wave and entered her family's restaurant.

Her dad was waiting in the doorway. "I know what you did, Alex," he accused. "You broke the rules and used magic because you wanted Riley to ask you out."

"I did no such thing!" She launched into classic autopilot denial—whenever accused by a parent, say you didn't do it. Then she smiled. "It totally worked."

"I don't think it did," her dad said sternly. He turned and walked toward the counter.

Alex hurried after him. "What are you talking about?"

"Your punishment?" her dad remarked calmly. "You're not going to the Fall Dance."

"What?" Alex shrieked. "Justin used magic! Where's *his* punishment?"

"Justin was already punished on the baseball field, when the other team ran around and around."

Alex's heart sank. All that planning and scheming, and now she'd be sitting at home while Riley took some other girl to the dance! Why does everything get all mixed up when I try to use magic? Alex wondered.

But at least she still had a date with Riley on Friday. She was sure that after that date she'd be his girlfriend. And if the date didn't go great, well . . . she could always try to use magic to fix it!

The next afternoon, when Justin walked out of the Sub Station's kitchen, he was surprised to see Kari sitting alone at a booth, sipping a soda. He tried to act cool.

"Hi, Kari," he said, walking over to her. She was wearing a pretty green sundress that brought out her eyes. Okay, now I'm getting nervous again, he thought.

"Oh, hey, Justin," she said, smiling. She looked happy to see him.

"Mind if I join you?" Justin asked.

"Please do," she replied happily.

Justin sat across from her and rubbed his hands together awkwardly. Now is the time, he thought. I'm a baseball hero. It's not going to get any more perfect than *now*. He took a deep breath. "So I was wondering, since you like baseball players and everything, if maybe you'd not want to not go to a movie or something."

Kari gave him a curious look. "Did you just ask me out?"

Justin blushed. "I think so. I was trying to." Here comes the humiliation, he thought.

"Oh. Okay. Sure. I'd love to go to a movie with you."

Justin was totally ecstatic. But he forced himself to try to act nonchalant. He had a date with Kari! "Excellent. So we're on. This weekend. Uh, what movie do you want to see?"

"Oh, I only date baseball players, and I only see movies about—"

"Baseball," Justin finished.

"No, cats," Kari replied.

"*Okay*," he said slowly. Not what he was expecting, but he could work with it. "Uh, are there any movies out right now about cats?"

"No," Kari replied sadly.

"Uh-huh." Justin could feel the chances of a date beginning to slip away. He needed to think fast. "Uh, would you see a movie about dogs?"

"Not unless they're cats disguised as dogs," she said.

"Farm animals?" Justin asked hopefully.

"Are the cats, like, disguised as farm animals, like, cows and stuff?" Kari asked.

And that was when reality hit Justin harder than a fastball to the chest. He and Kari weren't really a great match. Sure, she was cute and friendly, but they didn't really have much in common.

"Yeah. I'll tell you what," Justin said, getting up from the table. "Why don't we wait until a cat movie comes out? I'll keep an eye on the paper. Real close. Good talking to you, Kari."

Then he turned and headed toward the kitchen. Wizard classes with his dad started in a few minutes. He'd be early. Maybe practice a few spells. Spells were a lot easier to figure out than girls—at least for now!

PART TWO

Chapter One

Justin Russo paced the family room, ready to take action. He had a clipboard tucked under his arm and a whistle hanging around his neck, so he was very prepared. He checked the clock. Twenty minutes had passed since his parents left the apartment. It was time. He glanced at his little brother, Max, who was sprawled on the sofa reading a comic book. His younger sister, Alex, sat cross-legged on the floor. Justin picked up the telephone.

"Hey, Mom," he said when his mom answered her cell phone. "Okay, so you and Dad crossed over into New Jersey, right?" His parents were spending the afternoon at farmers' markets, buying organic tomatoes, lettuce, and other veggies for the Waverly Sub Station, the sandwich shop that they owned and ran. Justin grinned when his mom said they were long gone from the city. "Then it's official. I'm in charge," he said proudly.

But his mother didn't agree. She wanted to know why someone needed to be in charge. All three kids were old enough to be left home alone.

Justin sighed and nudged Max's foot off the back of the sofa. Max grunted and buried his head deeper into his comic book. "Because what if there was a tidal wave or something?" Justin asked.

Alex rolled her eyes. Justin could be so dramatic sometimes!

"I know, I know," Justin said to his mom. "But if there was, then would I be in charge?" He waited for the verdict. "Yes!"

Justin hung up the phone and blew his whistle. "All right. I'm in charge."

Suddenly, ice-cold water splashed all over him! Justin jumped back in shock. Alex had pelted him with a water balloon!

"Oh, look, a tidal wave," Alex said, unable to control her giggles. "Now you're in charge." She turned to Max, and they bumped fists in celebration. Justin was such an easy target.

"Not funny, Alex," Justin sputtered. "This is my new sweater." He gestured toward the blue-and-navy-striped sweater he was wearing.

"Justin, when you wear it every day for a week, it's not new, it just needs a wash," Alex informed him.

But before Justin could respond, he was

ambushed by another water balloon. Water soaked his left sleeve, dripping onto the floor.

"Okay. I washed it," Max joked, doubling over in laughter. He gave Alex a high five. "You're welcome."

Alex laughed along with Max. She would have thought that playing pranks on Justin would be getting old by now. Funny thing was, nothing could make her and Max laugh more.

Alex stood and straightened her denim miniskirt that she was wearing over her red footless tights. "Oh, well, have a good day, guys." She headed for the front door. "I'm out of here."

"Alex! Where do you think you're going?" Justin demanded.

"I'm meeting Riley at the street fair," she told him.

"Uh, you're not going to the street fair. And you have to listen to me, because Mom and Dad left me in charge," Justin announced.

"Justin, most sixteen-year-old boys have fun when their parents leave town," Alex explained.

"Being the authority figure *is* fun." Justin grabbed Alex's arm and led her back to the sofa. He pulled a sheet of paper from his clipboard. "Now, I've prepared a wizard-training review sheet on some spells that I feel Dad hasn't covered enough in class." All three siblings had secret magical powers that they had inherited from their dad. It definitely made their lives interesting! He handed the sheet to Alex.

She skimmed the page. "*Murrieta-animata*? I know this one. It's the one that makes you think you're the boss of me."

Justin grimaced. "No. *Murrieta-animata* is a spell for making an inanimate object come to life."

"Thanks. That's the answer." Alex stood and tossed the paper back to Justin. "Well,

I'm done with my review." She walked to the front door, stepped out, and called over her shoulder, "See you later."

Justin watched the door swing shut. Alex made him so frustrated. Didn't she understand he was in charge? Why did she always have to break the rules? He knew she'd regret it. He wasn't sure how or when. But he knew she would. Hey, maybe a tidal wave *will* hit, he thought. Then she'd really be surprised!

Alex didn't give a second thought to ditching Justin. She headed toward the street fair to meet up with Riley. Even though their first date was a total disaster, Riley still wanted to hang out with her. Thank goodness, Alex thought. I really like him so much!

When she spotted Riley, they smiled at each other. Then they walked through the crowded street, which was lined with all kinds of cool booths and food carts. Alex told him all the latest gossip. "And then Jessica Miller told Marianna O'Shaunnesy that I shouldn't be able to get out of gym if no one else could, so then Marianna said that to—" Suddenly, she noticed that Riley wasn't listening. Not only was he not listening, he was checking out Marianna, who was walking by! She smacked his shoulder. "Riley!"

Riley whirled around. "What?" he asked innocently.

"You were staring at Marianna O'Shaunnesy!" Alex exclaimed.

"I wasn't staring!" Riley replied adamantly. "Alex, why do you always get so jealous? I was just looking, that's all."

"Just looking, huh?" Alex crossed her arms in front of her. "As in, just browsing? As in, doing a little shopping around? What are you in the market for, Riley?" she taunted. "A new girlfriend?"

But Riley had tuned Alex out. He was staring

at someone across the street. "Hey, honey!" he called.

"You're doing it again!" Alex could hear how shrill she sounded, but she couldn't stop herself. They'd been going out for a few weeks. What was he doing?

"Honey! Honey!" A guy in a bee-in-a-honeypot costume walked by and handed Riley a honey straw.

"He's giving out free honey samples," Riley explained. "I mean, come on, Alex, this is crazy." He sounded exasperated. "I don't think we should go out anymore."

"What? You're breaking up with me?" Alex couldn't believe it. Sure, she'd been secretly dreading this moment since they first started dating. But she'd never *really* thought he'd do it. "But we're so good together. I mean, we have so many good memories. Remember you, me, and the penguins at the zoo?" She waddled down the street like a penguin.

"What are you doing?" Riley asked.

"I'm acting out our favorite memories," Alex said, the desperation obvious in her voice. "And that one time when we went for a walk." She took long, exaggerated strides in front of him. "And then we went down the stairs." She pretended to descend a flight of stairs. She was sure if he could visualize the good times, then he wouldn't want them to end.

"Alex, I'm breaking up with you," he repeated.

"Okay, I'm not a very good mime. I'll admit that," Alex said.

"No, it's because you are constantly jealous," Riley explained.

"I'm *not* constantly jealous. I just really like you," Alex told him. Why can't he see that? she wondered. If I didn't like him so much, I wouldn't care who he looked at.

Riley shook his head. "Well, you have a

funny way of showing it." He headed down the street.

"No, I don't!" Alex shouted. "I'm constantly jealous. That's how I show it!"

As Riley continue to walk away in the other direction, Alex blinked back tears. She couldn't believe Riley had broken up with her. They were so good together. All their friends said so. She had to get Riley back.

But how?

Chapter Two

"Okay, I'm done with my wizard homework," Max told Justin. He handed his paper to his older brother. "Can I watch TV now?" He hopped off the sofa and looked for the remote control.

"Sit," Justin commanded. "Let me check it." He sat in the chair next to the sofa, pulled the pencil off his clipboard, and studied Max's work. "Uh-huh. Uh-huh. Uh-huh," he said after reading each answer. "Hmm. Yes." He handed the paper back to his brother. "You might want to look at spell number five."

"I got spell five wrong?" Max asked.

"No. Spell five is the only one you got *right*," Justin said.

Max stuck his tongue out. "You're meaner than Dad."

"Thank you." Justin decided to take this as a compliment. His dad was a good magic teacher. "Okay. You need to think harder about the *Murrieta-animata* spell. If you leave animated objects animated too long, then they develop emotions."

Max picked up one of Justin's boxed action figures from the coffee table. Justin *loved* action figures. "You mean if I turn this doll into a person, it'd feel bad about being stuck in the box?" Max asked, waving the box in the air.

"Don't touch that!" Justin cried. He

74

snatched the box from Max. "That's Calico Woman in her Legion of the Superladies uniform. They only made a thousand of these lovely ladies." He looked at the box lovingly. "Isn't that right, Calico Woman?"

No one in my family understands my collection, Justin realized. Not only was each action figure worth a lot of money, but each had a personality, a story, *and* a fabulous superpower. He knew so much about each figure, they felt like friends.

"So what you're saying is, there's nine hundred ninety-nine other guys who couldn't get a girl to talk to them," Max joked.

"Don't listen to him," Justin whispered to Calico Woman. His brother had a lot to learn—about magic *and* about action figures!

"Riley broke up with you?" Harper's eyes widened. Her best-friend radar had immediately sensed something was wrong when Alex ran over to her in line at one of the street-fair food carts.

"Yeah, but I'm being really strong." Alex's lip quivered.

"Well, that's good." Harper reached for the sugary doughnut stick the man in the cart handed to her. "You want some churro?"

"Sure." Alex suddenly burst into sobs. "Riley used to buy food and let me eat some of it," she said sadly.

Harper nodded sympathetically. "You guys were so good together." She just couldn't imagine why Riley would dump Alex. "Remember that time you went to see the penguins?" She waddled like a penguin for a few steps.

Alex cringed at Harper's charades. "Oh. That did look weird," she said, remembering when she did the same thing in front of Riley. How many other weird things did I do in front of him? she wondered.

"Hey, Alex," a voice suddenly said.

She looked up to see Ken Walsh from her math class standing in front of her. He was holding Lane Redmond's hand. They had been dating for almost a month.

"Uh, I heard that you and Riley broke up." Ken nervously brushed his blond hair off his forehead. He gazed at Alex longingly. "What do you say you and I go out?"

"Um, *excuse* me, Ken?" Lane asked haughtily. "Hi. Uh, we're going out." She raised her hand, which was still holding his. "Like right now."

"Yeah, I've been meaning to talk to you about that," Ken said casually. He smiled at Alex. "This will only take a second. Wait for me." Then he pulled Lane a few steps down the street to talk to her alone.

Alex rolled her eyes. She'd laugh if she weren't so sad about Riley. "I can't *believe* Riley thinks I'm jealous," she complained to Harper. Then her despair quickly changed to anger. "You know, Riley would be jealous, too, if I were looking at other guys all day," she pointed out. Suddenly a plan started to churn in her head. A plan to get Riley back.

"You know what you should do?" Harper said. "You should have an open and honest talk with Riley to establish trust. Then, you'll have a firm foundation for the future."

"Ew." Alex stepped back in disgust. "That sounds like something old couples in their twenties would do."

"Then what are *you* thinking?" Harper asked.

"I'm thinking I'll find a boyfriend who's cuter than Riley, make him jealous, and then he'll want to get back together with me," Alex said.

"Yeah." Harper smiled. That did sound like a good plan! "What am I thinking? We're not in our twenties." She and Alex laughed.

"So, see any cute guys around here?"

Harper asked as they walked through the fair.

Alex scanned the street. A bunch of guys from school, no one really . . . and then she spotted him. He was tall, with dark hair. Alex stared. He was perfect. There was only one teeny, tiny problem. He wasn't alive. He was a mannequin in a store window!

So what if he's just a mannequin, Alex thought. A little magic can cure that.

The first thing she had to do was distract Harper. "Hey, Harper, did you see that booth where they sell rock families with the eyes glued on them?" Alex asked.

"Where?" Harper squealed. She absolutely loved rock families. They were so incredibly adorable!

"Around the corner where—" Before Alex could finish her sentence, Harper dashed off in search of the rock families. Alex glanced around. No one was watching. She quickly climbed into the display window. Reaching into the sleeve of her shirt, she pulled out her magic wand and pointed it toward the cute mannequin. "*Murrieta-animata,*" she chanted.

There was a quick flash of bright light. Then the mannequin moved. He stepped stiffly off his platform.

"Ow. That pole hurts," he said.

"Well, hello, handsome," Alex greeted him with a grin. She tucked the wand back into her sleeve.

"Hello to *you,*" he said. The mannequin seemed surprised to hear his own voice. "Hello. Hello. I can say hello. *Why* can I say hello?"

"I'll explain that later." Alex figured it was better not to get into the details. "The important thing is, I'm Alex and your name is . . . Manny. Yeah, Manny. Last name Kinn. Manny Kinn." That's good, Alex thought. Real good. "Okay. And you're my new boyfriend."

"Whoa. This is moving too fast. I just got off that pole!" Manny protested.

Alex grabbed his hand and pulled him from the display and out into the street. "Let's go!" she exclaimed excitedly.

Just wait until Riley sees me with my new boyfriend, Alex thought. It was time to begin Operation Jealousy.

Chapter Three

Alex and Manny walked through the busy street fair. Manny stopped every few seconds to gasp at the amazing sights. A stop sign. A hot dog. A miniature poodle. He couldn't believe how awesome the world was!

Alex searched the crowd for Riley. She wanted to walk by casually with her new boyfriend. Let him check out Manny. But she didn't see him anywhere.

She sighed and bought a can of soda from a street cart. Flicking open the top, she handed the can to Manny, offering him the first sip.

Manny inspected the shiny metal can, then lifted it and poured the soda over his head!

"No!" Alex grabbed the can. She forgot how little Manny knew about the real world. She ripped the paper off a straw, popped it in the soda, and handed the can back to him.

Manny smiled, then poured the soda on his head again.

Yikes! Alex reached for the can and, at that moment, spotted Riley standing by a booth that was selling T-shirts. He was definitely watching her.

Alex pretended not to know Riley was there. She opened a second straw, pushed it into the can, and then snuggled close to Manny as they both sipped the soda, cheek to cheek.

A little while later, Alex spotted Riley sitting at a table outside a pizzeria. Riley pulled a newspaper open and acted as if he were reading it. Alex totally knew he was watching her and Manny. Score!

"You know, you look so familiar. Where do I know you from?" Manny suddenly said.

Alex whirled around. Who was he talking to? Oh, no! Manny was a having a conversation with a plastic pizza-guy statue by the front door of a pizzeria.

"You know, you look just like my uncle. But they took him away a long time ago." Manny didn't seem to realize that the plastic statue wasn't alive. "I mean, that's okay, because, I mean, it was just me in the window then for a while."

Alex grabbed Manny and pulled him down the street. She couldn't imagine what Riley was thinking. They stopped in front of a plastic duck game. The ducks floated in a circle in a small pool. Manny clapped his hands in delight. He pulled a pink plastic duck from the water and presented it to Alex.

"Uh . . ." Alex was getting a little freaked out. She turned to leave and spotted Riley poking his head out from behind a row of stuffed animals at a nearby booth. He was spying on her. Her plan was working!

Alex turned back to Manny. She accepted the plastic duck and smiled at him.

Meanwhile, Harper headed into the Waverly Sub Station, searching for Alex. She hadn't been able to find her again at the street fair. She hoped she wasn't off in a corner depressed about Riley.

But Alex wasn't in the restaurant, so Harper sat down next to Max and placed a box on the table. She pulled off the lid and showed him her new rock family nestled inside. "This is my mom, my dad, my grandma, and me," she explained.

"Your dad's a *pirate*?" Max peered closely at one of the painted little rocks.

"Oh, my gosh! One of my dad's eyes fell off! Nobody move! Nobody move!" Harper screamed. She dropped to her hands and knees, searching the floor for a tiny googly eye.

Max got up and walked away from Harper. She's on her own with this one, he decided. He sat next to Justin at the counter. Justin was wearing science-lab goggles and plastic gloves. He was cleaning the side of a doll's box with a cotton swab. "What are you doing?" Max asked.

"I'm cleaning Calico Woman, because I'm selling her on the Internet. Well, her and Man Boy. Even the box has to be in mint condition." He rubbed off a small fingerprint. "Oh, by the way, did you clean your room or just shove everything under the bed?"

"Cleaning my room *is* shoving everything under the bed. That's why beds have an underneath," Max told him pointedly.

"Hey, everybody," Alex called as she and Manny entered the restaurant. He had a bewildered look on his face. "This is my new boyfriend, Manny."

Manny stepped up to the counter. "Hey, everybody." He smiled proudly. "I can say hello."

"Uh, hello. I'm Justin." Justin held out his right hand. But Manny totally ignored it and walked away. Strange dude, Justin thought. "Uh . . . Alex. What happened to Riley?" he asked.

Alex rolled her eyes. "We broke up, like, an hour ago. Where have you been?" Brothers were a little slow when it came to relationships, Alex realized.

Alex looked at Justin and smiled. "After grieving over Riley for fifteen minutes, I met Manny and it was love at first sight," she told him. She turned to her new boyfriend. "Right, Manny?"

"Right," Manny agreed.

Just then, Alex cringed. Manny had taken

several straws out of the canister and stuck them behind his ears. He looked ridiculous! "No," she mouthed to him as she removed the straws.

Manny grinned. "I didn't even know what it was like to feel alive until I met Alex," he told Harper, who was still crawling around the floor, trying to find her rock dad's missing eye.

"Aw, that's so sweet. You guys make such a cute couple," Harper cooed. "Alex, it's like Manny was made for you!"

"You have no idea," Alex quipped, nervously watching Manny inspect the salt shaker. "Manny, this is Harper."

"Nice to meet you. I'm looking for an eye," Harper explained.

"Oh." Manny raised his hand toward his face.

"No." Alex batted his hand away. She pulled Manny back toward the counter. "And my brother, Max. And my older brother,

Justin. And those are Justin's dolls." She pointed to the pile of display boxes on the counter.

"Found it!" Harper suddenly cried. She stood up, holding a tiny speck between her fingers. She peered at, it then shook her head. "Oh, this isn't my dad's eye. It's a button." She examined it more closely. "Wait, buttons don't have legs. It's a bug!" She screamed, dropped the bug, and bolted out the door. She bumped into Riley, who was just walking in.

Riley watched Harper run by and then slowly walked into the restaurant. "Alex. Can I talk to you for a second?" he asked.

"I don't know." Alex was playing it cool. She didn't want Riley to know how happy she was to see him. "Manny and I are pretty busy talking about how I don't get jealous, but"— she glanced at Manny stuffing napkins into his mouth and quickly changed her plan—"sure."

She followed Riley to a booth in the corner.

"I feel horrible about our breakup. I was stupid," Riley admitted. "I didn't know what it felt like to feel jealous until I saw you with that guy over there." He nodded his head toward Manny, who was now pelting cotton swabs at Max and Justin.

"His name is Manny," Alex said. Riley is *so* cute when he's apologizing, she thought.

"I prefer to call him 'that guy over there,'" Riley grumbled.

"What are you saying, Riley? You want to get back together?" Alex asked.

"I would. Yes," he admitted.

"Well, I don't—" Alex wanted him to sweat it out a bit. One . . . two . . . That's long enough, she thought. "Okay."

"Really?" He looked relieved. "Well, what about 'that guy over there'?"

"Oh, don't worry. Manny's used to being 'stood up.'" Alex laughed at her joke. Then she noticed Riley's confused expression. "It's a—

it's an inside thing," she tried to explain. "Stood up." She chuckled. It was too bad Riley couldn't appreciate her fabulous sense of humor.

She led a happy Riley out the door, promising to meet him back at the fair in a few minutes, and found Manny sitting alone at a table playing with the sugar packets. She guessed Justin and Max were in the kitchen. There was no one else in the restaurant.

"You're breaking up with me?" Manny asked, having overheard her conversation.

"Yes. And you're okay with it because I'm going to turn you back into a mannequin," she said brightly.

"All right," Manny agreed.

She slipped her wand out of her sleeve. She pointed it toward Manny and said, *"Garibay-immobilitay."*

But Manny continued to sit there smiling, looking exactly the same. "Huh?" Alex wasn't sure why the spell hadn't worked. "Okay, one more time. *Garibay-immobilitay*."

But nothing happened. Her spell wasn't working. Manny was the same as before. She still had a living mannequin.

She noticed Justin coming out of the kitchen. "Excuse me. Stay," she told Manny. She cornered her brother. "Uh, Justin. A question, completely out of the blue. What's the spell to unanimate something you've brought to life?"

"*Garibay-immobilitay*," Justin replied.

Alex shrugged. "Oh. Well, I tried." She walked back to Manny and gave him a huge smile. "So, Manny, this is your lucky day. You're free to live your life. You'll do great out there, a handsome kid like you." She grabbed his hand and guided him toward the door. "Okay. You enjoy." She waved as she gave him a push out into the bustling streets.

"All right," Manny said agreeably.

Alex sighed and closed the door behind him. Problem solved.

"You know, that's too bad," Justin said as he watched him go. "I really liked Manny. Oh, and he wears the same sweater as me, which I saw on a mannequin . . . that looked a lot like Manny . . . Kinn." A strange look passed over Justin's face. "Manny Kinn," he said slowly. "Manny Kinn," he repeated, faster this time. Then it hit him. "*Mannequin*," he said with a sigh.

"Yes. I animated the mannequin from the store!" Alex cried. "What's the big deal?

"Alex, you can't be using magic without my permission! That's a complete disrespect of my authority," Justin scolded.

"Hey, I tried to change him back, but it didn't work!" Alex said defensively.

"Uh-oh." Justin looked wary.

"What 'uh-oh'?" Alex asked. Judging from Justin's expression, this was bad. Big-time bad.

"If you bring something to life and it develops emotions, you can't change it back," he explained. "Manny's in love with you."

Alex gasped. What? This was *so* not what she had in mind! What was she going to do now?

Chapter Four

Alex couldn't believe what she had just heard. She tried to play it cool. "Don't be ridiculous. He's a mannequin! He can't be in love with me," Alex told Justin. She laughed at the thought. She left to find Riley. It was time to enjoy the street fair with her *real* boyfriend.

Ten minutes later, she and Riley were sitting at an outdoor table, holding hands. As she gazed into his brown eyes, an enormous bouquet of red roses suddenly appeared in front of her.

"Alex, look, I brought you one flower for every minute that I've loved you," Manny declared.

Alex gaped at the beautiful roses. There were at least a hundred of them! "Oh, no." She had a terrible sinking feeling. Justin was right. Manny *was* in love with her!

She pushed the roses toward a shocked Riley and jumped up. "Manny, we broke up, don't you remember? You have to stop following me." She was trying to be as nice as possible.

"I can't, Alex. I'm in love with you. You get me. You taught me how to drink from a straw without poking myself in the eye. Remember the time I kissed the duck?" He smiled at the memory.

Alex felt terrible. Manny sounded just like she had when she was trying to hold on to Riley. She tried to think of a solution, a way not to hurt Manny's feelings. Then it came to her. "But what if someone else got you?" she asked him. "And then you could have even better times with them."

"Really? Do you know that someone?" Manny asked.

"I think I do." Alex smiled. Her plan was inspired. "She's a real doll. She's a friend of my brother's."

Alex cracked open the front door of their apartment and peeked in. She could see Justin and Max at the kitchen table. She sighed in frustration. Her plan would have to wait until later.

Alex watched as Justin handed a dusty old book to Max.

"More wizard homework? Dad doesn't even make me do homework on Friday!" Max protested.

"Max, if you put it off until Sunday night,

then I won't be able to put you kids to bed early. Have a little quiet time for myself," Justin said as he steeped a tea bag in his mug and paced around the dining-room table.

"What are you going to do, light some candles and take a bath?" Max mocked.

"My quiet time is my quiet time," Justin said defensively, sounding just like his mother.

Max stood up. He'd had enough. "Okay, so you're a teenage boy who drinks tea and likes to take baths." He smiled mischievously. "Like I'm not going to tell anyone about that on the Internet." He laughed and bolted upstairs for the computer in his bedroom.

"Hey! You get down here, young man!" Justin blew his whistle and chased after him. "That's it!"

Alex pushed open the front door. She heard her brothers' feet pounding up the stairs as she snuck inside. She knew she only had a few minutes before one of them came back down.

She had to work her magic quickly.

She tiptoed to the kitchen counter and grabbed the box that contained Calico Woman. Sliding the doll out of the box, she bent it so it sat on the edge of the counter. Taking a step back, she pulled out her wand.

"Okay. *Murrieta-animata*." And to make her bigger, Alex added, "*Grande!*"

Bright lights flashed, and suddenly a woman dressed in a black unitard with leopard-print trim and a headband with cat ears stood before her!

"Ow! Oh, those twist ties really hurt," Calico Woman exclaimed, rubbing her wrists.

Alex grinned. Instant girlfriend. She grabbed Calico Woman's arm, brought her outside to the street fair, and spotted Manny. Perfect!

"Manny, meet Calico Woman," she said, introducing them. "Calico Woman, meet Manny. You two have a lot in common."

Manny looked at Calico Woman, who had long golden hair, talonlike nails, and a serious expression on her face. "I don't have anything in common with a superhero!" he exclaimed.

"Oh, you're so wrong, Manny," Alex said. "Who likes to say hello?"

"Ooh, ooh, ooh!" Manny raised his hand and jumped up and down. "Hello."

"Hello," replied Calico Woman.

"Who here is dishwasher-safe?" Alex asked.

Calico Woman waved her razor-sharp nails. "That's the only thing about me that's safe," she hissed.

Alex forced a smile. "See? You two are going to be so happy together." She pushed them toward each other and retreated to Riley's side.

"I'm still in love with her," Manny confessed to Calico Woman, gesturing toward Alex.

"Oh." Calico Woman gave a slight shiver. "When you say that, that makes me really mad."

"Yeah, that's called jealousy," Manny explained.

"Oh!" Calico Woman gasped. "I don't like that feeling."

"There. See? All done," Alex told Riley as they watched the new couple talk. "He's perfectly happy with her. Now nothing can go wrong." Yikes. She knew that bad stuff always happened when she said things like that. "Oh, I hope I didn't jinx that," she added nervously.

Chapter Five

"And right after dinner, you have to take a shower and then get into your pajamas," Justin instructed Max. Justin was liking this whole being-in-charge thing.

"Can I take a shower *in* my pajamas?" Max asked.

"Then you would be wet, your pajamas would be wet, and your entire bed would be wet," Justin pointed out.

"But if everything's wet, is anything really wet?" Max asked. Justin stared at his little brother, amazed. What was with his mind-bending questions? "Like when you're totally underwater, you're not really wet," Max explained.

"Yes, you are," Justin said, annoyed. Did his parents have this much trouble getting Max to do things? he wondered.

Justin walked toward the kitchen counter and then suddenly stopped short. A familiar empty box lay there, ripped open. He gasped. "Calico Woman's gone! Where—?" He frantically searched the floor.

Max picked up the box and inspected it. "Well, duh. It says right here, no chains can hold her." He pointed to the writing on the front of the box. "Chains are a lot stronger than a cardboard box."

"See?" Max ripped the box in half.

"Max! What are you—?" Justin squeezed

his eyes shut. So much for selling Calico Woman in perfect condition! Her box was destroyed, and she was missing.

"Alex!" Justin yelled. He knew she had to be responsible for this somehow!

Alex couldn't have been more pleased about how the day was turning out. She walked hand in hand with Riley down Waverly Place.

Just then, Manny raced up to them. "Alex, don't leave me! Look, look! I won you a stuffed gorilla!" He handed it to Alex.

She sighed. She thought Manny would be so happy with Calico Woman. Well, at least happy enough to forget about Alex. I guess I was wrong, she thought.

"All right. Enough. This has got to stop, Manny," Riley warned him. "It's over."

"But I'm in love with her," Manny said.

"Seriously! It's over!" Riley yelled. He began to chase after Manny.

"Wait!" Alex sprinted after them, still holding her stuffed gorilla. "Riley, wait!"

Calico Woman dashed behind her. "Manny, Manny! I love you!" she cried.

Meanwhile, Justin surveyed the street fair with Max. "Okay, let's split up and find Alex, because wherever Alex is, that's where my Calico Woman doll is."

"Well, there's Manny," Max said, watching the living mannequin run by.

"Oh, and there's Riley." Justin pointed to Alex's boyfriend chasing Manny.

Alex rushed past them, dragging the stuffed gorilla along the ground. She was only steps behind Riley. "Oh! Found Alex," Max called.

"Manny!" Max and Justin turned to see a woman in a black-leather catsuit running down the street.

"And Calico Woman," announced Max. "Man, she is huge!"

"*And* alive!" Justin exclaimed.

"Manny! Manny! We were both made in China!" Calico Woman's voice echoed down the street.

Justin began to run. He had to catch his doll!

Manny wove through the fair. He dodged kids with cotton candy and people eating funnel cakes. Riley hopped on an abandoned scooter and zoomed after him. Alex ditched her stuffed animal, strapped on a helmet, and borrowed a demonstration skateboard to give chase. Calico Woman followed behind her. Justin, desperate to catch up, spotted a clown on a miniature bike. He pulled the bike away from the small clown and pedaled frantically, his knees pumping past his ears. The clown yelped and ran after Justin.

Manny tried to run faster. They still hadn't caught him, but they were getting close.

"We need a volunteer! Who wants to sit in the dunk tank?" called out a carnival guy in a blue-and-white-striped vest. He stood in front of a huge round tank filled with water.

"I'll go in!" Manny waved his arms as he ran through the crowd gathered around the tank.

"Excellent. Excellent. Just climb right up there." The carnival worker pointed to the platform perched above the tank.

Manny scrambled up and sat down on the platform. He hoped he'd be safe up there.

"Okay, who would like the first shot at sending this handsome fella into this dunk tank?" The carnival worker held up a beanbag.

"I would!" Riley skidded his scooter to a stop and grabbed the beanbag.

Alex jumped off her skateboard. "Riley! What are you doing?"

"I'm going to teach Manny that no one comes between me and my girl," Riley declared.

Alex giggled. Riley really *does* like me, she

thought. She was so distracted thinking about Riley that she didn't see him throw the bean-bag. It hit the target squarely, releasing the platform and plunging Manny into the water.

"No!" Calico Woman yelled as she ran up to the platform.

"Alex!" Justin cried. He appeared just in time to see the big splash.

"Oh, no. What happened to Manny?" Alex took a hesitant step and peered inside the tank. This can't be good, she thought.

Chapter Six

The Russo siblings were nervous about looking in the tank. Finally, Max peeked in.

"It looks like he got wet," Max commented. "You know, sometimes water can make a spell wear off."

"How do you know that?" Justin asked.

"Because the spell just wore off," Max replied quietly. He pointed to Manny, who was now just a jumble of unassembled mannequin parts.

Calico Woman teetered over to the tank. "Manny, what have they done to you?" she wailed.

"What's going on here?" the carnival worker demanded.

"Alex, 'that guy over there' just turned into giant doll pieces!" Riley shouted.

"That's it!" the carnival worker barked as the crowd pressed closer to the tank, leaning in for a better view. "I'm calling Waverly Place street fair security!"

"No, no, no. No need to do that, okay?" Alex stepped forward, trying to calm everyone down. "Um, I have to tell you something. I have to tell everybody something." She stood in front of the tank to address the crowd. She was frantically thinking of something believable to say. "Ladies and gentlemen, the man you saw in the dunk tank is really a—"

"Alex!" Justin interrupted, rushing to her side. He was afraid she'd tell everyone they were wizards.

"Magician!" Alex finished.

The crowd gasped.

"The Great Manic-Keeny!" Alex exclaimed. Alex breathed a sigh of relief. It looked like the crowd was buying her story! "And for his big trick, he has disappeared in the dunk tank, leaving an unassembled mannequin in his place!" She reached into the water, pulled out an arm, and held it high in the air for everyone to see. "Ta-da!"

The crowd cheered enthusiastically. "Oh, yeah." Justin was impressed by his sister's quick-thinking save. He gestured toward Alex. "And how about a hand for his lovely assistant!" He clapped, and the crowd applauded even louder. "Yeah!" Then he noticed Calico Woman leaning over the edge of the tank. "Watch the outfit. You're going back in the box," he warned.

"I never liked you," she hissed. Then she raced off.

"Hey! Hey, you get back here!" Justin darted after her.

Max stared at the tank. "Wow. I thought Manny was just a mannequin who got turned into a person and then back into a mannequin. But he was really just a magician. Great show! Great show!" He clapped and cheered.

A little while later, Justin walked with Alex along a quiet section of Waverly Place. The street fair was closing down. The crowds had gone home. But Justin still hadn't tracked down Calico Woman.

He sighed. It had been a long day. "Look, Alex. See what happens when you break the rules?" he said.

"Things end up working out for me?" Alex asked with a knowing grin.

"No. You almost exposed us as wizards, and I lost Calico Woman. She was worth a hundred bucks," Justin griped.

"Hey, I got my boyfriend back, and I'll give

you a hundred bucks," Alex offered. "Who got hurt?"

"I did, because you didn't respect me being in charge," Justin said. He sat on the curb and looked down.

"Why is that so important to you?" Alex sat down next to him. "What about living? Having fun? Doing stuff to tell stories about? Like this. This is going to be a great story to tell."

"The only people you could tell the story to would ground you," Justin pointed out.

"If you would calm down every once in a while, I would tell *you* stories," Alex offered.

Justin nodded. He knew this was his sister's way of saying she was sorry without actually having to say it. That was okay with him.

"Like, I bet you always wondered what happened to your light saber and cape," Alex said casually. She got up and headed toward home.

"Alex!" Justin cried. "How am I supposed to calm down when you tell me stuff like that?"

He chased her down the street, wondering if there was a magic spell to stop sisters from annoying their brothers!

Something magical is on the way!
Look for the next book in Disney's
Wizards of Waverly Place series.

Oh, Brother!

Adapted by Heather Alexander

Based on the series created by Todd J. Greenwald

Part One is based on the episode "Justin's Little Sister," Written by Eve Weston

Part Two is based on the episode "Alex in the Middle," Written by Matt Goldman

Alex Russo sat in Mr. Laritate's social studies class, talking to her best friend, Harper Evans. She kept her eye on the door, waiting for the teacher to walk in. Just as the bell rang, he entered the classroom. He was dressed in his usual suit, but instead of a regular tie he was wearing a bolo tie, a traditional cowboy neckpiece. "All right my little history

115

wranglers, enough ruckus," Mr. Laritate bellowed. "Let's start off Thursday's class as we always do." He paused and waited for his usual punch line. "With an oral pop quiz!"

All the students groaned. Alex turned to Harper, who was sitting behind her. "Oh, my gosh," she commented sarcastically. "It's the Thursday pop quiz we have *every* Thursday. I'm totally caught off guard." She rolled her eyes.

Mr. Laritate scanned the classroom for the first student to call on. "In no particular order," he said, "Wendy Bott, you're up! The French and Indian War was fought by three groups of people. Name two of them."

Wendy stood up. She fidgeted nervously as she stuttered. "Um . . . the French was one for sure," she said. "And the other one . . . I'm just going to guess, Indians?"

Mr. Laritate grinned. "Excellent!" he exclaimed, as he rang the large cowbell sitting on his desk. He called on the next student. "Nellie Rodriguez, you're up. The War of 1812 started in what year?"

"Oh, my gosh," Nellie said nervously. "I studied for this one." She quickly looked down at her hand where she had written the answer. "Uh . . . 1812?"

Once again, Mr. Laritate rang his bell. "Another winner!" He zoned in on Alex. "Alex Russo," he said. "The Monroe Doctrine. What is it? When was it passed? And please give a two-minute argument defending it."

Alex couldn't believe it. Everyone else had gotten such easy questions! This was totally unfair.

"Hold on," she said, standing up. "The other two questions had the answers in them. My question's supposed to be: the Monroe Doctrine—whose doctrine is it? I'd say 'Monroe' and you'd say, "Yipee-dilly-willy-way-to-go-little-filly.'"

"Oh, Alex," groaned Mr. Laritate, shaking his head disapprovingly. "You are *definitely* not your brother Justin."

"No, I'm not," Alex agreed. "I'm cuter and more fun to talk to. And I don't have dental floss on a key chain."

Mr. Laritate reached for something in his pocket. "Yeah, well I do!" he exclaimed, pulling out a key chain that had dental floss hanging from it. "Justin made it for me." Mr Laritate let out a sigh. "Ah, Justin. Those were the days."

As Alex sat down, she turned back to Harper. "Can you believe this?" she asked. "He's comparing me to Justin."

"I know. It is so hard to live up to Justin," Harper said sympathetically. Then she got a dreamy look on her face as she thought about Justin. "He's smart and handsome, and he has the healthiest gums. I mean—"

Alex held up her hand. "Okay, I get it! He

118

flosses. Let's make him president!" She turned back around in her seat and slumped down in her chair. It was going to be a long social studies class!